Who did that?

Jill B. Bruce
Illustrated by Jan Wade

Kangaroo Press

1/4 size

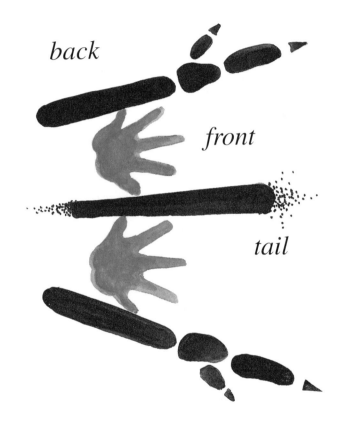

back

front

tail

2

Who did that?...

3

...An eastern grey kangaroo did!

If you see these tracks and droppings, you will know that an eastern grey kangaroo has hopped by. The feet and footprints of all kangaroos are a similar shape. There are two long prints made by the back legs, two small ones made by the front feet, and a longer print in the middle made by the tail. You can tell from the prints if the kangaroo was walking or if it was bounding away because it was frightened.

Kangaroos are herbivores. They eat only green vegetation, roots, tubers and fungi. Their dark green droppings are oval shaped. Four to ten pieces are usually found where a kangaroo has been feeding.

Eastern grey kangaroos (*Macropus giganteus*) are found in all states of Australia except Western Australia and the Northern Territory. Kangaroos belong to the *Macropodidae* family. Macropod means 'great foot' and all macropods have long back feet.

Male eastern grey kangaroos weigh up to 66 kilograms and grow to 230 centimetres long. Females are smaller and often weigh only half as much as males.

When they are born kangaroos are very tiny and poorly-formed. They look like little pink jellybeans. Soon after birth they climb up their mother's fur into her pouch, where they attach themselves to a milk teat. The baby kangaroo, called a 'joey', stays in the pouch for up to 12 months. When it is too big to climb into the pouch it still pokes its head in for a drink of mother's milk until it is 18-months-old.

Eastern grey kangaroos are quite common and are often a nuisance to farmers. They eat the grass on farms and destroy crops. It is illegal to capture or kill any macropod in Australia without a permit unless you are Aboriginal.

There are over 49 different members of the kangaroo family, from mouse size to over two metres tall. The red kangaroo (*Macropus rufus*) is the most widespread and one of the largest kangaroos. Four of the smaller species are threatened with extinction. The main reasons for this are: the land where they live is being cleared for farming; dingoes and feral foxes kill them; and rabbits eat the plants they feed on.

Full size

back

front

Who did that?...

...A koala did!

This is what you would see after a koala has been around. Koalas have very distinctive tracks and droppings. On their front paw, or hand, they have two thumbs and three toes, all with claws. Each foot has a clawless toe at the side, a second double toe with two claws, and two other clawed toes. Koala droppings are usually found beneath the trees they live in. The dark green droppings are a long oval shape with pieces of coarse fibre showing. When dry, they are very hard.

Koalas (*Phascolarctus cinereus*) are one of the world's cutest animals. They are often called koala bears, but they are not closely related to bears. They are marsupials, which means 'pouched mammal'. Unlike most other marsupials, the koala's pouch opens towards the back. Soon after birth the tiny baby crawls into its mother's pouch and attaches itself to a milk teat. It comes out of the pouch at six months and begins eating gum leaves. Koalas drink mother's milk until they are a year old. When the young grow too big for the pouch they cling to their mothers' back.

Koalas live in eucalyptus (gum) trees and eat over a kilogram of leaves a day. They are fussy eaters and only eat the leaves of 35 different types of gum trees. The name *koala* comes from an Aboriginal word which means 'does not drink', as koalas rarely drink water. Koalas grow up to one metre long and weigh up to 14 kilograms. Their thick fur resists cold better than most other animals' fur. Koalas can jump into water and swim very well.

There are three types of koalas: Victorian, New South Wales and Queensland. They are all slightly different. Koalas live in all states of Australia except the Northern Territory, Western Australia and Tasmania.

Koalas are a threatened animal as only 400 000 remain alive today. They are protected by law but many are killed by disease, dogs and traffic. In some places koalas cannot find enough food because gum trees have been cut down to make way for farms and houses. They could be extinct in 20 years if their habitat is not protected.

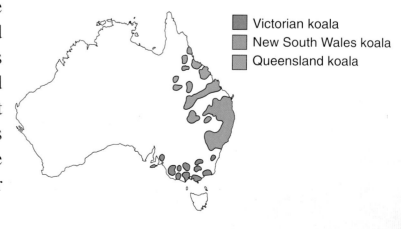

	Victorian koala
	New South Wales koala
	Queensland koala

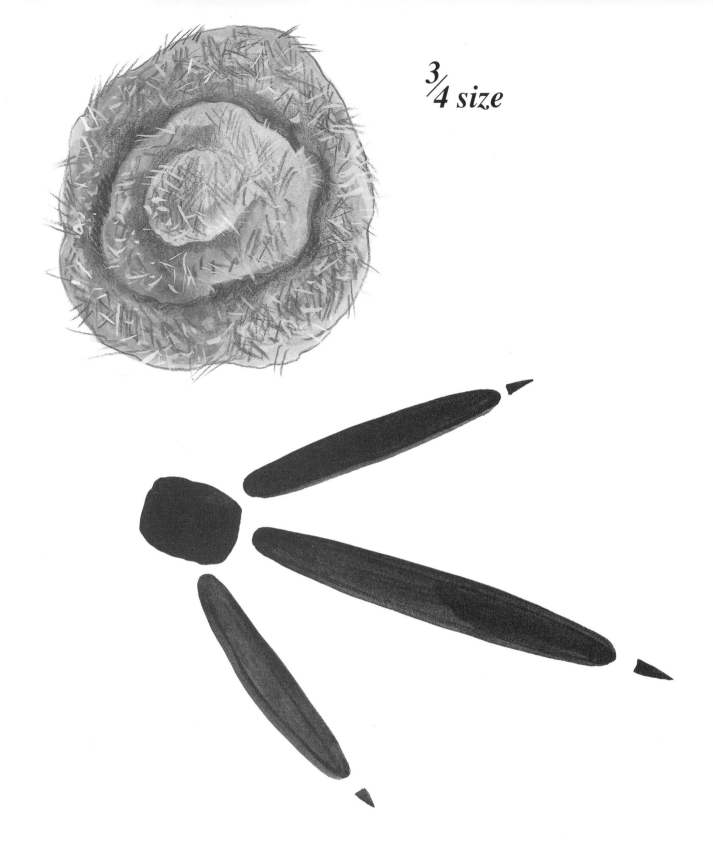

3⁄4 size

Who did that?...

...An emu has left its calling card.

Emus' large droppings are olive-green, sloppy and round. They contain a lot of leftover fibre from grass, seeds, fruit, flowers, caterpillars and grasshoppers. Emus' feet have a long middle claw or toe with two shorter toes on either side plus a small heel pad. Their footprints look a lot like a kangaroo's front footprints. You can tell the difference if you remember that emus run by placing one foot in front of the other and kangaroos hop with both feet together.

The emu (*Dromaius novaehollandiae*) is the second tallest bird in the world. Emus can grow up to 1.7 metres tall and weigh up to 50 kilograms. They cannot fly, but they run very fast. Their thick grey feathers hide two small wings.

Female emus joined women's liberation a long time ago. After the male builds a nest of grass, twigs and leaves, the female lays up to ten large green eggs. She then wanders away, leaving the male to sit on the eggs until they hatch eight weeks later. The father protects the small striped chicks and keeps them close for about eight months. If you see an emu looking after a clutch of chicks, it will be their father, not their mother. The stripes on the chicks fade away as they get older.

Emus live in lightly forested areas and grassy plains. They are found over a large part of mainland Australia. Sometimes emus are pests, as they break down fences and eat crops. In several places there are emu farms. Leather is being made from the emu skin and the meat is sold as a delicacy.

Half size

back   front

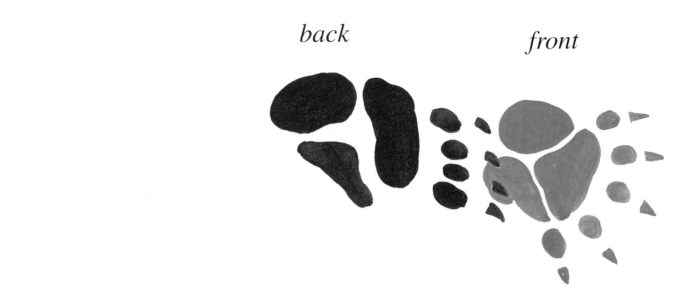

Who did that?...

...A wombat did!

It shuffled through here, leaving a trail of footprints and droppings. Wombats spread their dark green, cube-shaped droppings on rocks and sand. They scratch around them to mark out their territory. The four to eight pieces of droppings are made up of tightly-packed plant material.

Wombats' hind feet are like koalas'. They have a large clawless first toe and four other toes with claws. The front foot has a fleshy palm with five clawed toes. Wombat footprints are easy to recognise because their slow, ambling walk leaves heavy footprints with the toes turned in. The back feet often step on the prints left by the front feet.

Wombats are related to the Diprotodon, a huge prehistoric marsupial. Their closest living relatives are koalas.

There are three species of wombat: the common (*Vombatus ursinus*), the southern hairy-nosed (*Lasiorhinus latifrons*) and the northern hairy-nosed (*Lasiorhinus kreffti*). Common wombats have short ears and rough, thick brown to black fur. Hairy-nosed wombats have fine, silky grey hair and bigger and pointier ears. All have very short necks and tails.

■ Southern hairy-nosed wombat
■ Northern hairy-nosed wombat
■ Common wombat

16

These large chubby animals grow up to one metre in length and can weigh up to 40 kilograms. They have strong short legs which they use to dig large burrows. Wombats move great mounds of earth while digging their homes. They usually live alone and sleep all day. In the cool evening they come out to feed on leaves, grass and other coarse vegetation.

Like other marsupials, wombats give birth to tiny, immature young who crawl into the backward-opening pouch to feed on their mother's milk. They remain in the pouch for six months and stay near their mother for 18 months.

Wombats are found in all states of Australia except the Northern Territory. The common wombat exists in large numbers but it is estimated that only 40 northern hairy-nosed wombats live in a colony in Queensland. Efforts are being made to ensure they survive.

Full size

front

back

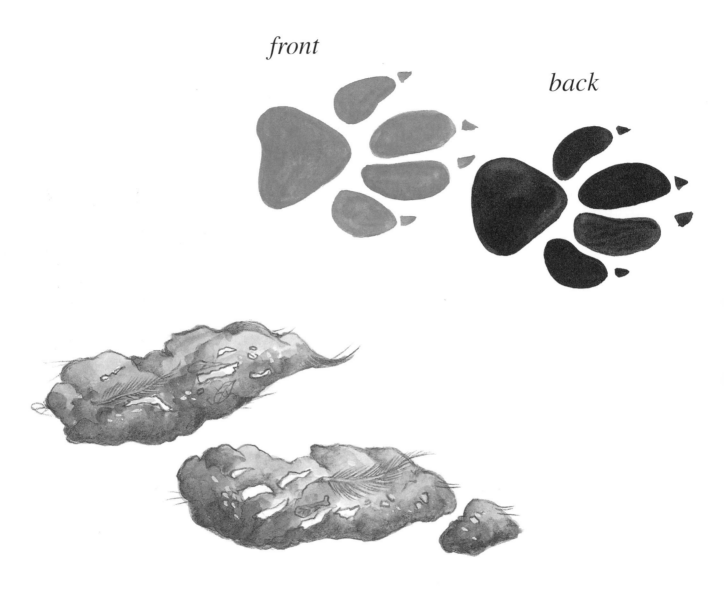

Who did that?...

...A dingo did!

Sometimes it is very difficult to tell who went by—a dingo or a large dog. Both have the same footprints and similar droppings. Each of their paws has four clawed toes and a pad. The front paws are larger than the rear paws. Dingo droppings have a really bad smell. They contain bone pieces, feathers and bits of insects, lizards and plants. The droppings are round at one end and pointy at the other. Pieces of animal hair show in the pointed end.

The dingo (*Canis familiaris*) was probably brought to Australia by Aborigines over 7000 years ago. The Aboriginal name for the dingo is *Warrigal*. These mammals are medium-size members of the dog family. Purebred dingoes have larger skulls and bigger jawbones than pet dogs. They have alert faces, ears that stay erect and bushy tails. They can vary in colour from yellow to sandy-red, brown or black.

Dingoes eat wallabies, rabbits, wombats, reptiles and farm animals like sheep and calves. They sometimes hunt alone but often hunt as a family group. Dingoes do not bark like dogs, but utter yelping sounds and mournful howls.

Dingoes give birth to up to eight blind, hairless young in their lairs in caves or dense bush. The pups drink their mother's milk for three months and then begin to hunt with their family group. If they are caught young enough, they can be trained to be good pets or working dogs. Dingoes are protected in the Northern Territory, but in other areas farmers shoot them because they kill calves and sheep. Dingoes kill feral rabbits and do less damage to the environment than the rabbits they eat.

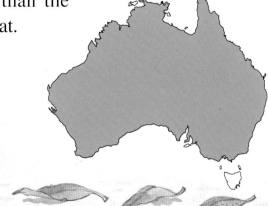

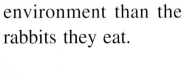

Full size

Who did that?...

...A fairy penguin!

That's who just waddled by in its best dinner suit. Fairy penguins are now known as little penguins (*Eudyptula minor*). They can leave two types of footprints: the first made when they waddle along putting one foot after the other; and the second when they jump with both feet together when they are frightened. Their webbed feet have three claws, or toes. The prints are a triangle shape with marks made where the three-clawed toes dig into the sand as they walk. Their droppings are usually a white sloppy patch with a dark centre.

Fairy penguins live on the coast of southern Australia and New Zealand. These funny little black and white birds are about 33 centimetres high and are the smallest penguin. Like all penguins they are unable to fly but they are excellent swimmers. Instead of wings they have flippers which they use as paddles in the water. All

penguins have short thick feathers which are white on the belly and black on the back. Penguins communicate with each other using a short yelping bark.

They eat fish—mainly pilchards and anchovies—and squid and krill. Each year fairy penguins moult, which means their feathers fall out and new ones grow. For the 15 to 20 days they are moulting their plumage is not watertight so they cannot go to sea.

Fairy penguins build their breeding nests in burrows. Large groups of their nests on islands and grassy headlands are called rookeries. Between August and October two white eggs are laid and both parents keep the eggs warm until they hatch after 35 days. One parent cares for the chicks while the other goes fishing at sea. The chicks feed by putting their head down their parent's throat. The parent then brings up the fish it swallowed at sea. When the chicks are between seven- and ten-weeks-old they go to sea for the first time.

Fairy penguins can live for up to six and a half years. At sea they are eaten by sharks and leopard seals. Some penguins are killed by oil spills and plastic pollution. On land pacific gulls, sea eagles, dogs, foxes, feral cats and humans are the chief causes of death.

Full size

back

front

26

Who did that?...

...A Tasmanian devil did!

If Tasmanian devils (*Sarcophilus harrisi*) live nearby, you will hear them in the night as they fight and scream over food. Look in sand for their unusual footprints. They leave a track of first one print, then two side by side, and then one print. Because devils are carnivorous their long, round droppings have a strong unpleasant smell. They contain pieces of fur, skin and fragments of bone. The droppings are usually found in the devil's lair or where it has been feeding on a dead animal's body.

Tasmanian devils live in the forest, woodland and farm areas of Tasmania. Fossil remains of devils have been found in areas of mainland Australia. This means they lived there thousands of years ago.

These marsupials have rough, thick black fur with white, irregular-shaped markings on the neck, chest and rump areas. They weigh up to eight kilograms and their body can be up to 60 centimetres long with a 25-centimetre-long tail.

Devils are nocturnal; they sleep in the day and hunt at night. They catch live prey such as small wallabies, rat kangaroos, birds and lizards. They will eat any animal

remains, or carrion, they can scavenge, even going onto beaches to find marine carrion. The devils' strong teeth and jaws make it easy for them to eat bones, skin and feathers. Devils have a whining growl which is followed by a snarling, snorting cough.

Tasmanian devils give birth to up to four young. The young attach themselves to teats in their mother's backward-opening pouch where they stay for 15 weeks. They are weaned off mother's milk at about seven months but stay with their mother for at least one year. Young devils are expert tree climbers but the adults are not so agile.

Tasmanian devils are quite common and are totally protected.

Full size

back

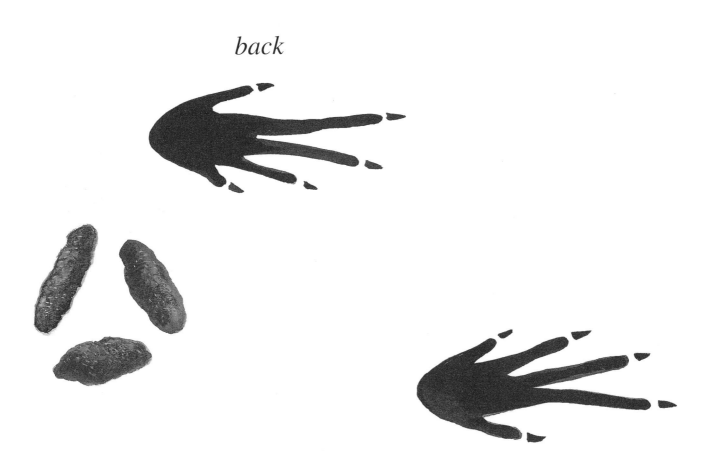

front

Who did that?...

...A frillneck lizard.

Frillneck lizards have five long claws on each foot. When they walk they leave four prints. If they are frightened they run away very quickly on their hind legs. Then they leave only two prints, one after the other. The colour and shape of their droppings changes according to what they eat. They are usually dark, oblong pellets containing pieces of insects and small animals.

The frillneck lizard (*Chlamydosaurus kingii*) lives in the warm tropical areas of northern Australia and southern Papua New Guinea. When alarmed this spectacular reptile stands with its head held high and raises the colourful frill around its neck. It then opens its bright yellow mouth and hisses loudly to scare its enemies away. This looks very frightening but is all bluff, as frillneck lizards are not dangerous or poisonous.

The frillneck lizard's rough scales can be pale grey, dark brown or speckled black. The frill can be patchy yellow, brown, orange or black. The muted colour helps them to blend in with the bark and leaves in their home in the trees. Frillneck lizards can grow up to 90 centimetres long.

Like all reptiles frillneck lizards are cold-blooded and cannot make their own heat. In the daytime they lie in the sun on branches, rocks or sand to get warm. They steal birds' eggs and pounce on small animals and insects for food. In January the female lays six to eight eggs and buries them in leaf litter. She then goes off and leaves the eggs on their own. When they hatch in eight weeks time, the young lizards must look after themselves.

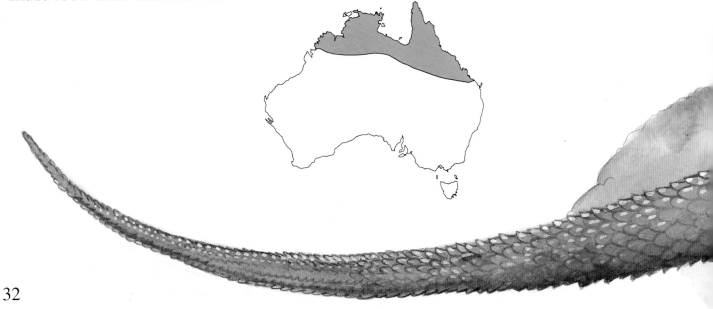

Full size

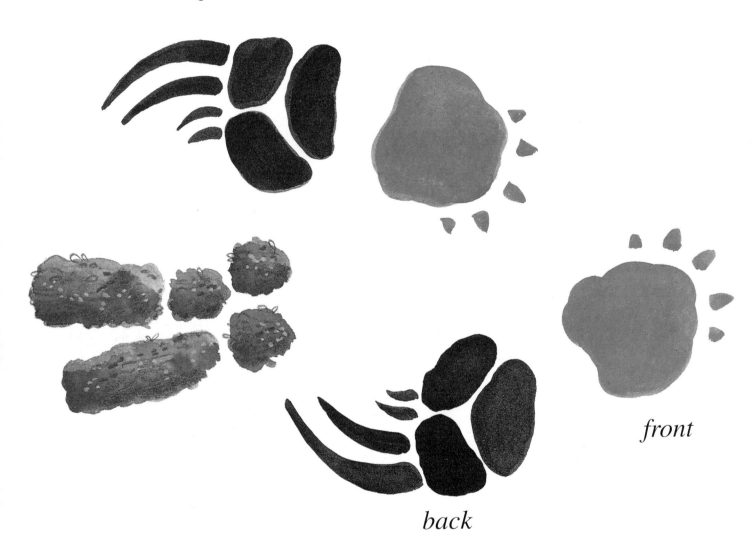

front

back

34

Who did that?...

...An echidna did!

The prickly echidna (*Tachyglossus aculeatus*) has a slow, shuffling walk. The two feet on one side of its body move forward together followed by the two feet on the other side. The front feet turn inwards and have five claws and a half-round pad. The rear feet seem to be back-to-front, with two large claws and three small claws facing backwards. Echidnas' long, round droppings are made up of pieces of insects and soil.

There are two types of echidnas, or spiny anteaters. The type found in Tasmania has more fur and less spines than the one found all over mainland Australia. These interesting animals are monotremes, or egg-laying mammals. The only other monotreme is the platypus.

Echidnas have a long tube-shaped snout and strong claws that they use to dig, poke and prod while searching for food. They lick up ants, termites and small invertebrates with their long sticky tongues.

Echidnas have poor eyesight but very good hearing. When threatened, they roll themselves into a round prickly ball or dig down into the earth. They have sharp cream-coloured spines growing out of reddish-brown to black fur. Echidnas grow to 45 centimetres long and weigh up to five kilograms. The males have a poison spur on each hind leg which can inflict a nasty wound.

In late winter or early spring the female lays one white, soft-shelled egg that hatches after ten days. The mother develops a temporary pouch on her belly. When the young grow spines at about ten weeks, the mother ejects them from the pouch. They feed on mother's milk until they can forage for food at about three months.

Echidnas do not have nest sites. They live in other animals' burrows or hollow logs, or just dig into the ground for warmth. They live in a variety of habitats ranging from dry semi-desert to lush rainforest. Echidnas are quite common animals and are not endangered but are wholly protected by law.

Full size

back

front

Who did that?...

...A numbat!

You would have to live in the bottom corner of Western Australia to see a numbat in its natural habitat. These rare marsupials have four claws on each of their small front and long back feet. Numbats move their back feet together and then lean forward to move their front paws together. If they move in a hurry they make a series of leaps. Numbats are very light. They only weigh 500 to 600 grams, so they do not leave distinctive footprints, only light scratches in the sand or earth. Their droppings are dark, oblong lumps which contain soil and remnants of ants.

The numbat (*Myrmecobius fasciatus*) is one of Australia's most beautiful marsupials. It has a long, flattened snout, head and body. Numbats have reddish-brown, black-tipped fur with white stripes on the back. The dark stripe around their eyes looks like a burglar's mask. They measure up to 40 centimetres, including their bushy brownish-grey tails which stand up in the air.

Unlike most marsupials, numbats are diurnal, or active in the daytime. They eat termites that they dig out of rotting logs and anthills with their forepaws. Numbats eat about 20 000 termites each day. They catch them by flicking their long, sticky tongues in and out.

Numbats do not have a pouch, so when the one-centimetre-long young are born they must attach themselves to the teats on their mother's belly. They then cling to the mother's fur for dear life. There are up to four young in each litter. Sometimes females build a small nest in a burrow or a hollow log. The young can look after themselves by the time they are six-months-old.

Scientists think numbats once lived all over southern Australia but there are now only 2000 left in the world. They live in hollow logs in white gum forests. If bushfires occur, the numbats are usually killed. Land clearing for farming has destroyed their habitat and feral foxes hunt them. Numbats are only surviving where areas of forest have been made into a reserve, with the foxes cleared out. Perth Zoo has a captive breeding program which will help ensure the numbat's survival and save it from extinction.

Full size

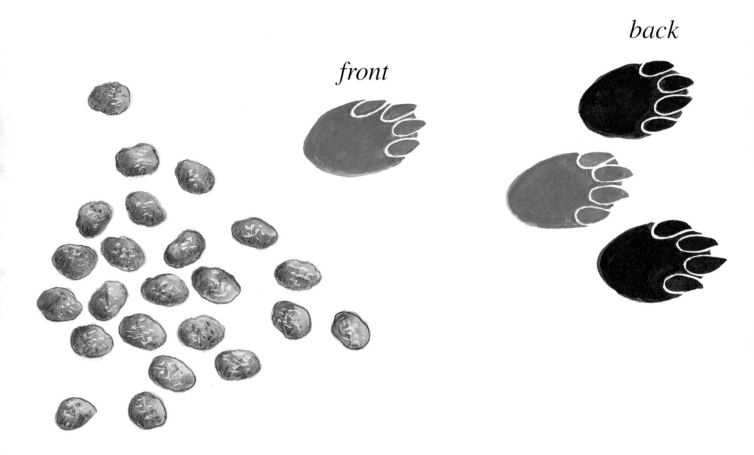

back

front

Who did that?...

...A feral rabbit did!

The farmer's number one enemy—a feral rabbit—has hopped by. The thick hair under a rabbit's feet leaves a round mark with four claw prints at the front. The larger rear footprints are nearly side by side, ahead of the two front prints which are apart, one behind the other. Rabbits use small heaps of their dark green, round, pea-size droppings to mark out their territory.

This fluffy little migrant, the European wild rabbit (*Oryctolagus cuniculus*), is a feral animal. Feral animals are non-native animals let loose in the Australian bush. Rabbits have been called 'the desert maker' because they eat all the plants and new seedlings. When the vegetation is gone, soil is destroyed by the forces of nature. Wind, rain and harsh sunlight soon make the land a lifeless desert where only sharp wire grass will grow.

Rabbits destroy the land by digging burrows or they take the burrows of native animals. They also eat the vegetation that native animals eat and use for shelter. This has caused many native animals to become rare, endangered or extinct. Rabbits eat almost any plants—grass, roots, shrubs or crops. They can survive for long periods without water as they get enough moisture from the vegetation they eat.

■ Found in these areas
■ Heaviest infestation

Rabbits give birth to a litter of three to seven young, which are called kittens. Females feed their kittens rich milk for about a month, after which the kittens feed on grass. They can have up to nine litters in a year but usually have about six. Young females, or does, can become pregnant when they are three-months-old so a pair of rabbits can have 70 offspring in six months. Rabbits live for up to three years.

Five domestic rabbits arrived in Australia on the First Fleet in 1788. By 1830 they were living in the wild in eastern and southern Australia and were pests to farmers. Then, in 1859, European wild rabbits were brought to Australia. They soon grew in number. In 1890 one farm was said to have 36 million rabbits on it.

In the early 1950s the disease myxomatosis was introduced into Australia and it killed up to 90% of the wild rabbits. Today the rabbits have built up a resistance to the disease and their numbers are again increasing.

Rabbits have caused millions of dollars of damage to the Australian environment. If feral animals such as rabbits, cats, foxes, camels, goats and buffaloes are not controlled, they kill off native wildlife and turn farmland into weedy deserts.

Keep your eyes open!

The first signs that an animal has been around, other than seeing the animal itself, are its droppings and footprints.

Droppings can also be called poo, dung, manure, excrement, turds, faeces, scats and sh..! Droppings is really quite a sensible name because the animal just drops its waste where it is standing or feeding. If you see dog droppings on your lawn, you know a dog has been there. If you see large round horse droppings, you realise a horse has been along.

By looking closely at droppings you can discover a lot of interesting things. If the droppings are warm and steam is coming off them, you know the animal has just left. If the droppings are fresh and soft, then you know it was not long ago. If they are dry and a light colour, then you know the animal left days ago. Droppings will also tell you if the animal is a herbivore (vegetation eater) or a carnivore (meat eater). Herbivore droppings have pieces of leaves, roots or grass in them and they don't smell too bad. But carnivore droppings have a strong, stinking odour. They contain bone fragments and pieces of skin and feathers.

Footprints are not always as easy to see, as animals may walk on leaves, rocks, grass or hard, dry soil. Prints can also be blown away by wind or washed away by rain. They usually only last a few hours.

Droppings and footprints can also tell you the size of the animal. Small dogs will have small droppings and small prints and big dogs will leave large droppings and large prints. Prints can also tell you if the animal was running, leaping, hopping or walking slowly.

Keeping your eyes open will help you discover a lot about the animals around you, their food and their habits.

Have fun! Keep your head down and keep on looking. You will then find out who really *did* do it in Australia!

Glossary

carnivore	An animal that eats mainly meat or flesh.
carrion	The rotting flesh of dead animals.
diurnal	Active in the daytime.
doe	Female rabbit, kangaroo or deer.
droppings	Excrement of animals.
extinction	When no more of an animal or plant are alive.
feral	Domestic animals let loose in the bush.
habitat	The natural home or area where an animal lives.
herbivore	Any animal that eats only plants.
invertebrate	Any animal without a backbone.
lair	The resting place of a wild animal.
macropod	Animals of the kangaroo family with large back feet.
mammals	Warm-blooded animals who feed their young mother's milk.
marsupials	Animals with a pouch for their young.
monotreme	Egg-laying mammal.
moult	To shed feathers or skin which is replaced by new growth.
myxomatosis	An infectious disease given to rabbits to kill them.
nocturnal	Active in the night time.

Index